Rose's Journal

THE STORY OF A GIRL
IN THE GREAT DEPRESSION

Power Man!

BY STEVE STRONG

MYSTERIOUSLY ENDOWED WITH THE STRENGTH OF FIFTY MEN, POWER MAN BATTLES THE FORCES OF EVIL.

MY POWER EYES ARE ALWAYS ON THE ALERT.

SUDDENLY...

HELP, OH HELP! MY FOOT IS CAUGHT ON THE TRACK, AND A TRAIN IS COMING! HEEEELP!

WILL POWER MAN GET THERE IN TIME?

YES! HE SWOOPS DOWN AND SNATCHES THE TERRIFIED GIRL FROM THE JAWS OF DEATH!

OH, POWER MAN, HOW CAN I EVER THANK YOU?

THANKS AREN'T NECESSARY. I'M JUST DOING MY JOB.

YES, WHEREVER HE GOES, POWER MAN LEAVES BEHIND A CROWD OF GRATEFUL PEOPLE. BUT LEAVE HE MUST — TO BE ALONE, ONCE AGAIN.

Photographs are rare for our family, but one of the programs started by President Roosevelt to fight the Depression pays photographers to go around the country taking pictures. A man, Mr. Rothstein, and a woman, Miss Lange, keep coming through our town. The good thing is, if they take your picture, they send you a copy.

Me, fetching water from the well. With this drought, the rain barrel's dry as stone. (Miss Lange took this photo even though you can't see my face.)

Rose's Journal

THE STORY OF A GIRL
IN THE GREAT DEPRESSION

Marissa Moss

Chicken and Steak Dinner
With hot biscuits and
cream gravy. All you **75c**
can eat for.......
At Lee's Place
3301 Oak Lawn   Ph. 5-2200
Owner, Lee of P K's

Silver Whistle

Harcourt, Inc.

San Diego   New York   London

To Debbie

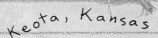

Keota, Kansas

This is what our farm looks like since the drought started three years ago. Mother had a big kitchen garden, and Father had acres of wheat and corn that turned golden in the summer. Now hardly anything grows, and the fields are just gray stubble.

I cut out of the Sears Roebuck catalog all the presents I wish I'd gotten. At least this way I can pretend to have them.

ROSE SAMUELS
11 years old

I looked at myself in the mirror to draw this picture.

china doll

January 1, 1935

HAPPY NEW YEAR! I sure hope 1935 is a heap better than 1934 — that was a dusty, dry, hot year, so I say good riddance to it. I can remember when Mother sang all the time, and Father told stories to Floyd and me after supper. I can remember when we'd have a big, beautiful fir tree filling the house with its piney smell for Christmas. But none of those things happen anymore. Times are too hard. Mother's always fretting. Father's too worried for stories. His face is like a door shut tight. And instead of a tree, we put some fir branches in a bucket and decorated them with old tinsel.

roller skates

We couldn't spare the 25¢ for a real tree, so we made do with what we could.

I wasn't expecting any Christmas presents. I know we can't afford anything. But when Grampa and Gramma came to visit, they gave me this journal. Floyd got one, too. It's a better present for him than for me. I like to draw fine, but I don't scribble everywhere all the time like he does.

story book

His ears stick straight out, and his hair sticks straight up.

Floyd wants to be an artist. He's 14 years old and still draws on the newspapers papering our walls.

January 3, 1935

Even in winter there's lots of work to do on our farm. I bring in the cows every morning to feed and milk them, then I feed and water the hogs, chickens, dogs, and cats. Last of all, I wash up and feed myself. Then Floyd and I walk the two miles to school. We're lucky the school's so close. A lot of kids have long walks and some have to get rides from their folks. Father's too busy to take the time to drive us. With nothing growing, you'd think he'd have lots of time on his hands. Instead he works twice as hard trying to figure out some way to grow crops in a drought and fatten cattle on thin straw.

Before the drought, our cattle were nice and fat.

Now they're skinny, with washboard ribs.

At school today the teacher, Miss Fisk, told us that the trial of the man accused of kidnapping and killing the Lindbergh baby has just begun. His name is Bruno Hauptmann, and his picture was in the newspaper, right on the front page. Miss Fisk said it's important news, but I don't see why. The trial won't bring back the baby. I feel bad for the Lindberghs, but it just seems part of the same hard times we're all in. Nothing goes right anymore.

Charles Lindbergh is famous because he was the first one to fly across the Atlantic Ocean.

The newspapers are packed with bad news — bank robberies, businesses closing, hungry men trying to scratch out a living by selling apples on street corners. Nothing seems to work right these days. It's bad times for everyone.

January 13, 1935

Father and Floyd had another big fight today. About farming, as usual. Floyd was drawing in his journal, and Father thought he should be doing chores (he'd finished already is all), so he yelled at Floyd for being a useless dreamer. "Can't eat those pictures you make, can you?" Floyd snapped back that farming's not filling our bellies, either. That really got Father mad! Even madder because it's true.

more flying news

This time when Miss Fisk read from the newspaper, it was more interesting. She said Amelia Earhart had flown solo across the Pacific Ocean from Hawaii to Oakland, California, in 18 1/4 hours. A huge crowd greeted her when she landed. I wish I could have been one of them. Or better yet, I wish I could have flown with her. The sky is so big, sometimes I tilt my head back and stare at the clouds until I feel I'm up there with them, not stuck on the ground. It's a great feeling. I bet flying is like that.

elia
rhart
amous,
I've
her in
sreels
the
ies.

January 18, 1935

I tried to help Father today when he went out checking fences to make sure nothing needed repairs, but he snapped at me to go back home and make myself useful. I _was_ trying to be useful! It's so unfair that he yells at _me_ when he's really mad

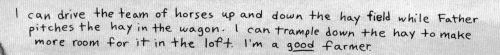

I can drive the team of horses up and down the hay field while Father pitches the hay in the wagon. I can trample down the hay to make more room for it in the loft. I'm a __good__ farmer.

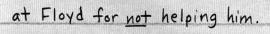

at Floyd for __not__ helping him.

Floyd's the one Father expects to take over this farm. Every year, Father lets him choose one of the heifer calves to keep, so Floyd can learn to care for his own herd. By the time he finishes high school, he'll have a good herd of breeding stock. Plus Father figures that if Floyd has his own cattle, he'll be more interested in farming. It hasn't worked so far, though Floyd __does__ care about his cows, especially the calf he picked last spring. He even gave her a name, Lulu, and he treats her like a pet.

He feeds Lulu out of his hands, but __real__ farmers don't name cattle and don't fuss over them. That's no way to raise cattle proper.

January 20, 1935

For supper last night we had onions boiled with salt and pepper, and biscuits with mustard. With all our cows, we should have plenty of butter, but Mother says we can't eat any. Instead we have to sell all we make so we can keep up payments to the bank for our farm. Would a little dab of butter make that much difference?

I dream of heavy chilled crocks of butter, butter melting on corn cakes, butter slathered on biscuits, butter dripping on beans. To think I used to eat butter ALL THE TIME!

I was feeling sorry for myself, going to school with nothing in my lunch pail but more biscuits and mustard, until I heard Miss Fisk tell my friend Pearl that she looked poorly and better get on home and eat something, she was like to faint from an empty stomach. Pearl said she couldn't, it was her sister's turn to eat. Imagine having so little, you can't even eat every day! I was so ashamed of what I had, I gave Pearl my lunch. (I admit I was happy not to taste that mustard again, but Pearl thought it was a real feast.)

January 26, 1935

Floyd, Pearl, and me went to the movies today. We watched Tarzan, Tom Mix, Flash Gordon, newsreels, and a Shirley Temple movie. Then we sat through them all again. The newsreels were about Bruno Hauptmann's trial in Flemington, New Jersey. The whole town is making money from it by selling souvenirs (like tiny ladders that are models of the actual ladder used to sneak into the baby's room). There were pictures of workers on strike, too, and more pictures (every newsreel has them!) of hungry men

Floyd loves the movies, but he loves the Sunday funnies even more. He says the stories are better and he copies the drawings for hours.

standing in breadlines. I wish they'd just leave the newsreels out. That's not the kind of thing I want to see at the movies. But Shirley Temple was great. She was a poor little girl who was really rich but didn't know it. She ended up in a beautiful house with hundreds of toys and servants bringing her whatever she wanted to eat. I liked the pony cart she had best, but Pearl liked the dollhouse. Floyd said he liked the movie because it was like getting out of Kansas, out of our lives, at least for a while. He said someday he'll really get out of Kansas. He wants to live in a big city, not be stuck on a farm.

I like the movies, too, and I like to imagine living somewhere else, but really, I love our farm too much to want to leave it. Even all dried up like it is now, I don't want to go. Tomorrow it might rain and be all green again. I love how wide-open everything is, how nothing gets in the way of the land. It stretches as far as you can see. And the sky arches over it all so close you feel you could touch an angel if you just reach out your hand. When the sun sets, it's like the whole world is filled with bright colors — the sky orange, yellow, and pink, and the ground deep purple shadows.

I try to paint it, but I can't get on paper what my eyes see. I can't even get close.

Mother uses flour sacks for everything — aprons, curtains, pillowcases, dresses, even underwear!

We trade different sacks with our neighbors so we can have matching patterns.

January 30, 1935

Floyd's last pair of socks wore clean out today. They'd been darned so many times, Mother said they were nothing but a passel of holes sewn together. But she's too proud to let folks know we can't afford socks, so she cut off the bottoms of Floyd's long johns and stuffed them into the tops of his shoes.

From the outside, it looks like socks, but inside the shoe, the feet are really bare.

Father laughed when he saw what she'd done, but it wasn't a happy kind of laugh. More and more, Father is low. Just when he thinks things can't get worse, he says, somehow they always do.

Now instead of telling us stories after supper, Father turns on the radio.

The radio is like the movies — I feel like I'm somewhere else when I listen to it. I wish the radio programs could cheer up Father, too. He listens but he doesn't seem any happier.

February 10, 1935

I like to hear comedians on the radio—Will Rogers, Jack Benny, George Burns, and Gracie Allen. Floyd likes the dramatic stories, the Phantom and Dick Tracy. But on Sundays we always listen to the same thing — President Roosevelt's fireside chats. Today he said that even though millions of men are out of work, the country will get through this Depression, because he's thinking of all kinds of programs to help people out. Mother said she'd starve before going on Relief. It's too shaming to ask the government to feed us. I suppose I should feel ashamed, too, but when I look in the larder and see nothing

Foods I dream about:

fritters

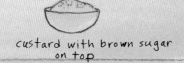
custard with brown sugar
on top

hot cocoa

except potatoes and onions, I wish Mother weren't so proud.
I'd love a bit of cheese and butter. I don't care who gives it
to us!

February 14, 1935

Bruno Hauptmann's trial is finally over. The jury took eleven
hours to decide, and two jurors cried as the sentence was read.
He's been found guilty and sentenced to die. Mother read me the
story in the newspaper, and, of course, at school Miss Fisk read it,
too. I still don't see why there's so much excitement about this,
but Mother said everyone loves Mr. Lindbergh because of all his
flying feats, and people feel sorry for him and his wife.
Besides, she said, when things are bad, it makes her feel better
to hear about people worse off than herself. I'm just the
opposite — when things are bad, I want to hear happy news
or at least jokes on the radio.

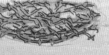

The newspaper had
a picture of a bird's
nest made of barbed
wire.

There are no stalks or leaves to build with
because of the drought, so the bird made do
with barbed wire. Now <u>that's</u> a sad story.

February 18, 1935

First came the Depression, then the drought, and now we're
having a heat wave. It's 75° in the middle of winter! I would
not mind the heat if only it would rain. As it is, the land is
dry and baked, and everyone's tempers are on fire. Father

I don't know my family anymore. Everyone's mad all the time. Are we drying up inside like our land?

Father  Floyd  Mother

and Floyd fight all the time now. It's time for spring plowing, so rain or no rain, hot or cold, Father went out this morning to plow the fields. He told Floyd to stay home from school and help him. Here's what happened:

Floyd: "My brains aren't scrambled from the heat. I'm not wasting my time digging in a graveyard, because that's what this farm is — a graveyard! We'll all be dead and buried in it!"

Father: "This here farm's fed and fattened you all your life, you ungrateful good-for-nothing! Farming isn't easy, but this land hasn't let us down yet, and it's not going to now. You just want an excuse to be lazy, to spend all your time with your foolhardy drawing. You don't want to help? Fine, but don't expect food from my table!"

Floyd: "I don't expect food! Boiled onions ain't food and bread soup ain't food, neither!"

I thought Father was going to hit Floyd, he looked so mad, but he just stomped off, slamming the door. I couldn't believe Floyd talked that way, so disrespectful and mean. That's not like Floyd, not the brother I know. Mother tried to make him apologize to Father, but he just stomped off, too, with more door slamming.

These are hard times for lots of folks, not just farmers like Floyd thinks. On the radio they had a dance contest where the couple that danced the longest would win $50. $50!! That's a fortune! People danced till they dropped, and the winning couple lasted seventeen days!

They practically danced in their sleep!

Floyd didn't help Father, but I didn't see him at school, either. Pearl says things are bad at her house, too. Her father hardly talks at all, and her mother just cries in the rocking chair all day, moaning that she doesn't know how she's going to feed her family. Pearl's even thinking of hopping a train out of here so her folks will have one less belly to worry about. I sure don't want her to go. With Floyd turned all mean and angry, she's my only friend. I've been giving her my lunch everyday at school so she'll want to stay. I'm sick of biscuits anyway. They stick in my throat.

The air should smell like apple blossoms and wild verbena, but all I smell is gray dirt. I have to draw them if I want to see them.

February 23, 1935

This is usually my favorite time of year, when green shoots and wildflowers carpet the ground, buds cover the trees, and meadow-larks sing early in the morning and late in the afternoon. But it's been six weeks since the last (short) rain, and nothing's growing. Everything's gray or brown. The only color is the blue of the sky, and even that's washed out.

Mother looks like all the color's been sucked out of her, too. She's hollowed out, all empty and sad. Father's not hollow, but he's hard and gray and cold as stone. Floyd's the only one

Motherlooks almost as old as Gramma now. Still somehow, no matter how little we have, she always manages to put something on the table for supper. No matter what Floyd says, we're not starving!

with any spunk left, but he's always angry and keeps to himself as much as possible. Today I followed him when he stomped off, and now I know where he goes when he wants to be alone—out behind the barn in the old root cellar. He was drawing his own comic page when I snuck up on him. At first he was mad at me, but I promised I wouldn't say nothing to Father about him spending his time with a pen instead of a plow. I wouldn't have anyway, even without promising, Floyd should know that.

He showed me his comic, and it was great! I liked it so much, Floyd gave it to me.

He told me he gets his ideas from real gangsters. He has a whole pile of newspaper clippings on Bonnie and Clyde, John Dillinger, Al Capone, and Pretty Boy Floyd (the bank robber, not my brother). There's even a picture of Bonnie and Clyde's bullet-riddled get-away car after they were killed in a shoot-out with government agents.

 What Pearl packed:

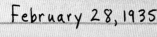 pots and pans

 comforts

 family album

bucket

February 28, 1935

I guess I can't complain about all our butter going to pay the bank, because at least we <u>own</u> our farm. Pearl's folks are tenant farmers, which means they pay for farming the land with some of the crops they grow. Because of the drought, they haven't harvested much, and now the company that owns the land is kicking them off. Pearl won't have to hop a train after all — her whole family is driving off next week. They're heading for California because there's supposed to be work in the fields there.

kerosene can to use as a stove

I want to give Pearl something, but I don't have anything. I asked Floyd if he'd draw Pearl a comic, and he said yes, if I'd write the story. So I'm writing one. I've never made up a story before, but I like it. I can see why Floyd does, too — you can make things happen the way you want them to, not the bad, sad way they do in real life.

rope

March 4, 1935

ax

Pearl is gone. Her family packed everything they own into their Chevy, and off they drove. They sold all their tools, but Father said so many farmers are leaving and selling off their belongings, the stores won't pay good prices. A plow that cost $18 from Sears Roebuck goes for 50¢, a seeder that cost $38 gets $2.

ivory letter opener from the Chicago World's Fair

Pearl's rag doll and our comic

Bible

clothes

lantern

Father wanted to help out and buy the cattle and horses, but we can scarce feed our own. Still, I took Pearl's dog, Rags, because she's about to have puppies and it near broke Pearl's heart to leave her behind. I wanted to do something for Pearl, and maybe if I have Rags around, I won't be so lonesome for my friend.

Pearl promised to write to me, but a letter costs 3¢ to mail and that's three more pennies than she has. I wish Pearl could just stay here with us. She could have all my food, I wouldn't care.

I'm glad I had the comic to give Pearl! She made me a yarn doll as a parting gift.

Mother knew the right thing to do. She had Father butcher a hog even though it's late in the year for that, and she made sausage and canned rib meat for Pearl's folks. She packed up biscuits and canned beans and tomatoes from last summer, and all together it was a real feast, more food than they'd seen in a long time.

We had real meat ourselves for supper — pork chops with biscuits and gravy. I should have been in hog heaven, but I couldn't take a bite because having pork meant Pearl was really gone.

Pearl with her
pa and brother,
fixing to go to
California.
When Miss Lange
took this picture,
I asked her
please, please,
please to
send me a copy.
And she did!
So I still have
something of
Pearl, her tiny face.

March 5, 1935

I guess it's good after all that Pearl left, because the dust storms have started again. I thought last year was bad, but this year could be worse. That's a horrible thought! I read in the newspaper last May that one storm was so big 350 million tons of soil were picked up from Kansas, Texas, and Oklahoma and dumped on the eastern states. 350 million tons! I didn't know there was that much dirt in all of Kansas! Chicago alone got 12 million tons (4 pounds of grit for each person in the city). In New York and Boston, the dust darkened the sky so much, street lamps were lit, even though it was daytime. The dirt traveled as far away as the Atlantic Ocean. Ships at sea were coated in Kansas dust!

Father jokes that you can tell a dust storm is coming by the sound of all the rattlesnakes sneezing. Ha, ha. I remember when Father told funny jokes. Even his sense of humor has dried up.

At the first sign of a duster, Floyd and I run to put all the water and milk in mason jars. We screw the lids on as tight as we can. Then when we're thirsty, we punch a hole in the lid and stick in a straw. If we try to unscrew the top, dust we can't even see gets into the water from the outside of the lid, and we end up drinking sludge.

That's how it is for us, all the time—dust just everywhere. Mother used to wash the whole house thoroughly everyday, but now she's given up. What's the point of cleaning, when the dust comes back, no matter what?

Floyd and I still try to keep things as clean as we can. Otherwise we'd go crazy! We've figured out little tricks to fight the dust — like if we coat our lips and nostrils with Vaseline, then the dust sticks to the Vaseline, and we don't breath or swallow as much grit. Even so, after a duster my teeth always feel gray with dirt.

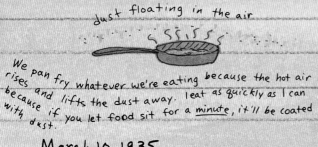

dust floating in the air

We pan fry whatever we're eating because the hot air rises and lifts the dust away. I eat as quickly as I can because if you let food sit for a _minute_, it'll be coated with dust.

To knead dough for bread, I put it in a dresser drawer and cover it with a cloth that has two holes cut into it. I put my arms through the holes and knead the dough that way.

I let it rise in the drawer (covered, of course) and whisk it into the oven as quick as I can. There'll still be some grit, but less than otherwise.

March 10, 1935

Yesterday was another duster, red this time. (Red means the soil comes from Oklahoma, gray means it's from Texas, and black is our own Kansas soil blowing away.) I had to scald the churn before I could make butter, and scrub out the wash-tubs before I could clean our dusty clothes and bedding.

I wanted Floyd to help me, but he was busy caring for Lulu. His pet calf (well, now she's a cow) was doing poorly. There's so little food and water. Now there's the dust adding to the animals' misery. The horses and cows have it worse off than we do. We can stop up the doors and windows with wet rags, but the barn's too open for that. Dirt blows in and covers the scarce straw in the mangers. It ruins the water in the trough. After a dust storm, all the animals are the same gritty color — they all wear a coat of dirt.

Floyd tried to coax Lulu into eating. He brought her fresh well water and a handful of precious oats, but she'd given up and wouldn't take anything. There was nothing he could do, but Floyd wouldn't leave her. He stayed with her all last night. It didn't make a difference. Lulu died early this morning.

Floyd hasn't asked Father for anything in a long while, but he asked for something last night. He wanted Father to save Lulu, to tell Floyd how to help her.

Father just shook his head and walked away. Floyd thought Father was being mean, but I saw tears running down his cheeks. Father wanted so much to do something.

Floyd didn't cry, but he hasn't said a word since. He sits like a stone and stares into space. For a minute I was scared he was turning into a dried-up old man, but I looked again and he was just Floyd, just a sad, sad boy.

Mother thinks it's all Floyd's fault, anyway, for turning a farm animal into a pet. She helped Father turn Lulu into steaks, but the truth of it is, she was so skinny, the meat's not good for much. When Father opened Lulu's stomach, it was lined with a thick layer of dirt. I sure hope my insides aren't like that!

I've swallowed my share of grit, too. I wonder if I swallowed a watermelon seed now it could actually grow.

dirt and more dirt

March 15, 1935

The day started clear and fine, so Floyd and I set in to planting potatoes. It used to be that when we did chores like that, Floyd would pass the time telling me about comics. Or about the gangsters he reads about. Not anymore, not since Lulu died. It's like a part of him died, too, the part connecting him to the farm, to us.

So it wasn't much fun digging. It was definitely too quiet. And then the quiet became something else, something thick and heavy, and before I knew it, there was so much dust swirling in the air, I could scarce see my own feet. Floyd yelled to get in the house, but I couldn't see where to go. A black sleet was all around me. Even if I could see, I had to close my eyes to keep out the stinging dirt. I was trying to figure out what direction I'd been facing and where the house should be when I felt Floyd grab my arm and pull me after him.

We stumbled into the house, coughing up wet wads of grime. Mother tried to clean us up, but even inside the house, the air was a gray haze.

Mother dosed us with a mixture of honey and turpentine to clean out our throats. More likely to poison us, I thought, but I remembered Lulu's coated stomach, and drank it up.

Father was out plowing. (Plowing in what? There's no soil left, just dust and more dust. We eat, breathe, and wear dust. That's the crop we harvest!) We waited for him to come home, but I guess it's so black he couldn't find his way. I hope he's somewhere safe.

 Mother tried to turn on the radio, but all the dust created so much static electricity it wouldn't work. Not being able to hear other voices, to be part of the outside world, made me feel like we'd been swallowed by a giant whale. But however bad it is for us, it must be worse for Father.

March 16, 1935

The storm's still kicking up dust, but Father's home! He said he couldn't see a thing when the storm hit. He floundered around for hours until he bumped into a fence rail. That was good luck! He just followed the rail to the barn. He stayed there until a break in the dust showed him the house, and he ran for it. He coughed up so much grit, it looks like he swallowed an acre.

We live in a desert now with dirt mounded up like snowdrifts. Stubble pokes through, but there's nothing green, nothing alive.

March 18, 1935

That last storm was a bad one. A little boy was lost in the dark dust and when the sky finally cleared, he was found suffocated. Another child got tangled in a barbed wire fence, but survived. A lot of our neighbors are taking it as a sign to go. Half of the town is boarded-up from merchants leaving, half the farmhouses are

I finished reading the book I got from the library. It's called The Wizard of Oz by L. Frank Baum. It's about a girl from Kansas, just like me. Only a twister blows her house away to a magical place called Oz. If only a duster would blow me to someplace like that!

abandoned.

When Pearl left, I never thought we might go, too. Now I wonder if we will. I hate this dust, this drought, this nightmare! But more than that, I hate the idea of leaving our home.

March 19, 1935

Some new life actually survived that awful duster. Rags had her puppies! I found them when I went to sweep out the barn (it's more like shoveling out). The puppies are so adorable, I wish I could keep one — or at least give one to Floyd. Maybe a puppy would make up for Lulu's death.

This is my favorite puppy. I named her Dusty since when I first saw her, she looked like a dust ball with eyes. I asked Father if Floyd could have her. I was sure he'd say no, but he said yes! I guess he sees how low Floyd is and wants to cheer him up.

March 20, 1935

I told Floyd I had a surprise for him and when he closed his eyes, I set Dusty in his lap. She licked his nose, and his face shone with the brightest smile! (It's been ages since I've seen Floyd smile. None of us smile anymore.)

Floyd rubbed his cheek against Dusty's soft fuzz, and I thought everything would be alright after all. Like Father always says, "Farmers live on hope, on tomorrow." And tomorrow will be better than today.

Dusty's tongue tickled Floyd's ear.

March 21, 1935

I thought Floyd was happier here because of Dusty, but he says he's had enough after that last duster. Now he wants to leave, too. He keeps arguing with Father that we should go to California, like Pearl's family and the Hudsons up the road, like so many of our neighbors already have. But Father won't go. This farm was his daddy's and his granddaddy's, and he won't be the one to give up on it. He insists that farmers expect bad years, but good times always follow. You just have to be patient. There's always another season, another crop if we can just keep going. But Floyd's not a farmer. He's never been a farmer. Father can't see that, but I can.

Floyd's given up on the land and he's given up expecting anything from Father.

Father doesn't give up so easy, not on the land and not on Floyd. He still thinks Floyd will wake up one morning and _be_ a farmer.

Mother doesn't say anything during these conversations — I can't tell if she wants to go or stay. Probably stay. How can she leave Gramma, Grampa, and Uncle Victor, who live three farms over, or Uncle Ned, who lives on the other side of the county?

And me, I don't know what I want. I'm scared to go and scared to stay. Maybe what some say is true — these storms are signs from God telling us to leave. All this darkness must mean <u>something</u>.

Even covered with dirt, our farm is beautiful. Mr. Rothstein, the photographer, must think so, too, or he wouldn't have taken this picture.

I was born in this house, and I always thought I'd be here forever. I can't imagine being happy anywhere else.

March 24, 1935

At first there were just a few, then dozens, then hundreds. Now there are _thousands_ — thousands of jackrabbits have come down from the hills, searching for _something_ to eat. I looked out the window, and it was like the ground was moving, jumping all over. Then I realized it wasn't the ground at all, but jackrabbits, so many you could scarce see any land between them.

So there's a new sport now, "rabbit drives." The men and boys all join together, herding as many rabbits into a pen as they can. When the rabbits are trapped, they're clubbed to death with old ax handles, sticks, brooms, anything. I hate it! I cover my ears, but I can hear the rabbits screaming. It sounds just like a baby crying, a cry of pure terror.

One or two rabbits are cute, but thousands of them are definitely creepy. Still I wish they didn't have to be killed.

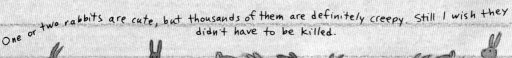

It's too dangerous to use rifles since the rabbits run in all directions, and you might shoot another hunter by mistake. Besides, there are far too many rabbits to waste bullets on.

At first Floyd didn't want to go along. "Butchering bunnies," he called it. Father said they were starving, anyway. It was a mercy to kill them, and at least we'd eat better. I guess he convinced Floyd (for once!), because the two of them went out to join the other men. And for once, I was glad to be a girl and stay home. Maybe it is a mercy, but it sure doesn't feel like one.

When the drive was over, there were cartloads of dead rabbits — far too many to skin and eat. I felt too sick to swallow a bite anyway.

Mother put her face in her hands when Father told her, next week there'll be more rabbits to kill.

I tried to comfort her by saying I'd help cook them. And I will, too, so long as I don't have to eat them. I don't think I'll ever eat rabbit again.

March 26, 1935

Floyd is gone. Even Dusty couldn't keep him here. He didn't say good-bye, just snuck out, leaving this note behind.

I'M SORRY, I CAN'T BE A FARMER. I'VE NEVER WANTED TO BE A FARMER. ALL I WANT TO DO IS DRAW, SO I'M HOPPING THE NEXT FREIGHT TRAIN TO CHICAGO, AND FROM THERE I'LL CATCH A TRAIN TO NEW YORK. I'LL WRITE TO YOU WHEN I GET THERE. DON'T WORRY, I'LL BE FINE. SINCE I CAN'T BE A HELP TO YOU, I DON'T WANT TO BE A BURDEN.
FLOYD

He left this picture, too, of him and Dusty in front of the house.

This photograph is all gray, but that's how everything looks now — just different shades of gray.

I miss him something terrible. Father says little, Mother says less. All I have is this journal to confide in — and Dusty.

It's been twelve days in a row of dust storms. I can't blame Floyd

Dusty looks at me with her big brown eyes as if she understands just what I feel. As if she's asking, too, "Why did Floyd leave us? Doesn't he love us?"

a bit for leaving even if I wish he'd stayed. Then I wonder if we're crazy not to go — if we'll all be buried in dust one day...

I can write my name with my finger in the dust on the windows — and I still wash them everyday.

The dust has kept me home from school, but today I went. It felt strange to go without Floyd. His best friend, Jack, came up and gave me his Buck Rogers decoder ring. "Send it to Floyd," he said. "Tell him I miss him."

Buck Rogers spaceship loo like this. I wis I could fly to Floyd in it.

I'm wearing the ring until I see Floyd again. It makes me think of him.

April 1, 1935

If it wasn't for the radio, I'd feel like the world was one big pepper shaker, and I was a little grain of pepper inside it. Father's wheat crop is long gone now. At least Mother has somehow kept her kitchen garden alive. Between dusters she waters the tomatoes, cucumbers, watermelons, potatoes, and beans. She wipes the dirt off the leaves and feeds the ground with eggshells and chicken manure. Father takes it as a sign not to give up, that we can still grow things here. Our farm isn't dead, and we won't let it die.

April 14, 1935

beautiful buttery sunshine

After so many gray days, today dawned clear and fresh, and I thought Father was right — there's hope for us here. It was such a beautiful day, everyone wanted to be outside. Mother and I did a wash, and it was a pleasure to hang the clothes in the bright sun. The sky was a soft blue, with big cottony clouds — the kind of sky that makes you feel close to the angels.

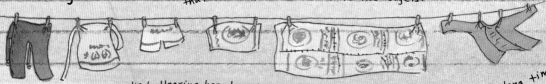

Mother even sang as we worked. Hearing her, I realized I haven't heard her sing in a very long time. She used to sing the whole day through.

Father thought it wasn't too late to try for a second crop of wheat, so he decided to sow the seed he'd saved. There still was no rain, but the sun was enough to give us all hope.

When we finished hanging out the wash, the day was so fine and Mother was so happy, we decided to take the horses and visit Gramma and Grampa. It looked like everyone was on the road, paying visits or having picnics, like we were all celebrating our good fortune in simply having the gift of a normal spring day.

If the fields had been green and thick with wildflowers, everything would have been perfect!

As we got closer to Grampa's farm, the air got suddenly colder, much colder. The sky was thick with quiet, and then there was the sound of thousands of birds, more and more each moment, as if they were trying to outfly an invisible monster. It was that same eerie feeling you get before a twister.

There were so many birds, they blocked the sun, a dark cloud themselves.

Mother yelled at me to hurry — we had to get to Grampa's. We kicked up the horses, but they were so skittish and fretful, I could barely get Flit's nose pointed in the right direction. Mother's horse, Lucky, was worse — she reared up and threw Mother off. I jumped off Flit to help Mother, and in a flash both horses were gone, racing off in a panic. Mother wasn't hurt, but we were both plenty scared. The wind was rising.

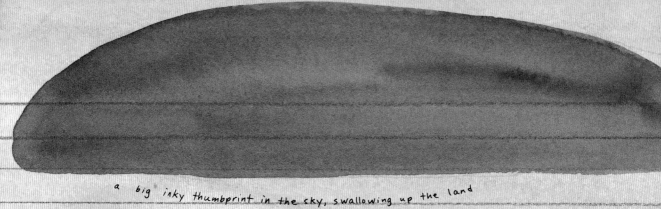

a big inky thumbprint in the sky, swallowing up the land

On the horizon we could see a great black smudge. Mother grabbed my hand and we ran. I've never been so scared, trying to outrace that giant black hand stretching out toward us. The wind pushed us forward, and just as we got to Grampa's gate, the first bits of dust whirled around us. We were so close, but it only took seconds for darkness to fill the air. I couldn't see, I couldn't breathe, I couldn't cry. All I could do was hold on to Mother's hand as she pulled me along. I choked on the thick, gritty air and squeezed my eyes tight shut to keep out the stinging dirt. The roar of the wind filled my ears and I thought, "I should have gone with Pearl, with Floyd, with anyone."

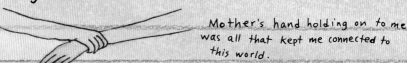

Mother's hand holding on to me was all that kept me connected to this world.

I don't know how she found her way, but over the howling wind, I heard a pounding — it was Mother pounding on wood, pounding on the farmhouse, pounding as hard as she could, until Gramma opened the door and we blew in along with buckets and buckets of dirt. Gramma slammed the door shut, and only then did Mother let go of me. We were both coughing and gasping, tears streaming out of our eyes.

It was pitch-black outside the windows, and I could still hear the wind and feel it shaking the house. I was shaking myself— I couldn't stop. Grampa brought some water, and Gramma washed the black off our faces. I should have felt safe then, but the whine of that wind terrified me and I could see the dust <u>inside</u> the house eddying and swirling around. What if the house blew away like in the story of the three little pigs?

It's a sturdy wooden farmhouse...

but it bends in the wind...

until it blows away

POP!!!

and it doesn't fly to the land of Oz!

Grampa said I shouldn't be scared — we're tough farmers. Hadn't I heard about the farmer who fainted when a drop of water struck him in the face and had to be revived by having buckets of dirt poured over him? Or the woman who saw a farmer buried up to his neck in dust, and when she asked if the man needed help, the farmer answered he was fine because he was on his horse.

I'm just hunky-dory.

That joke (Ha ha!) made me think of Floyd and his comics. I wonder how he is, what he's doing right now. One thing's sure — he's gotta be better off than we are.

I know Grampa was trying to cheer me up with his jokes, but I didn't feel any better. I've heard people say that all this dust means the end of the world is coming and we're being punished for our sins. I didn't believe it before, but now I wonder. What's happening now is like the Ten Plagues God sent to Pharaoh in the Old Testament. Last year we had frogs when all the ponds dried up, then jackrabbits, now darkness.

April 15, 1935

I scarce slept a wink last night. I kept getting up to rinse the grit from my lips, with water that was already dirty brown. We lay with damp washcloths over our noses to keep the dirt out and stayed as still as possible, since every turn stirred up a new cloud of dust from the blankets.

sleeping— I mean, trying to sleep— with washcloths over our faces

The only thing that made me feel better was thinking of Floyd. I imagined him someplace sunny with a beautiful blue sky, happily drawing his pictures. As long as he's free of dust, a part of me is free, too.

Floyd must be somewhere that has trees with green leaves, flowers, and air that tastes of sun and grass, not dirt.

Mother was eager to get back

The dust is thick, heavy, and dark— not like sand at all, but like earth whipped into the air.

home. She was worried about Father and our horses, but so much dirt had silted up against the house, we couldn't open the door. Grampa finally climbed out the kitchen window and shoveled the door clear. When we stepped outside, it was so horrible, I wanted to run right back inside. Hills of dirt mounded where the ground had been flat before, and all around were the stiff, dead bodies of birds, field mice, and jackrabbits — all caught by the dust and suffocated. If Mother hadn't found the farmhouse, that would have been us, too.

Grampa tried to start the old Ford, but there was so much dirt in the motor, it wouldn't catch. I went with him to hitch a team to the wagon, and my heart nearly broke to see the poor horses. The dust had mixed with the tears in their eyes to form a mud that cemented their eyelids closed. Frantic at being blinded, coughing up black grime, they were in no shape to go anywhere. I helped Grampa wash their eyes and noses as gently as I could, but I couldn't help wondering why God had to punish innocent animals along with wicked people.

Grampa looked so sad and old, I asked him if he wanted to pack up and leave like everyone else.

He was quiet a long time. Then he said, "In all my years, I've never seen anything like this, but I'm too old to go. I've gotta stay. I've just gotta." Does that mean we've gotta stay, too?

April 17, 1935

We finally made it home today. Father was safe — he, too, had seen the duster coming and had made it to the house in time. Our neighbor Mr. Moore wasn't so lucky. He was in his DeSoto and couldn't see where he was going. He drove the car off the road and choked to death on dust. Mrs. Moore won't stay here anymore. She's packing up her children and leaving, before she loses anyone else to this dark plague. That makes our neighbors on both sides gone. Will we be the only ones left?

The car was buried in dirt, as if it had been caught in a black snowstorm.

All that's left of Mother's garden.

Mother cried when she saw her garden. It had survived so many dusters, but not this one, not Black Sunday, as people are calling it. It wasn't the dirt but the wind that killed the plants. The air was so full of static electricity, it burned the plants black. But I felt worse for the animals. We lost 23 cows. At least Lucky and Flit made it to the barn safely, though I'm sure I don't know how they found their way in all that darkness.

I read in the newspaper that the temperature dropped 50° that afternoon, with winds of 70 mph! That's definitely supernatural weather.

Rags and Dusty survived fine, too. With a name like Dusty, that puppy will be the last one to die in a duster — I hope.

April 19, 1935

The Red Cross gave out dust masks at school for all children to wear. I hated putting it on — it's as suffocating as the dust! But Miss Fisk insisted we all wear them, so I did. Maybe I'll forget mine at home tomorrow.

The Red Cross also set up an emergency hospital — there have been so many cases of

a gift of the Red Cross

"dust pneumonia" (three kids in my class alone)! Mother doses me with Hunt's Lightning Oil Liniment, H.& R. Cough Syrup, and skunk grease. They all smell nasty and taste even worse, but they've worked so far. (Mother doesn't know, but I'm giving some to the dogs as well.)

skunk grease - I'm not sure what it really is (oil from a skunk?), but it sure stinks!

April 20, 1935

   Father read in the paper that folks have formed a "Last Man's Club" in Dalhart, Texas. The people in it pledged to stick it out, to stay and keep trying, no matter how bad things get. Father liked the idea so much, he decided to start his own Last Man's Club.

Father is in the middle. The club is pretty small, but Father's sure new members will join. I hope so — else there'll be just six families left in Keota, Kansas (seven really because Grampa joined the club even if he missed having his picture taken by Miss Lange).

   The wind has blown 27 days and nights without stopping. It's driving people crazy with the constant noise, the threat of new storms. Mother looks more worn and haggard than ever. She's not joining the Last Man's Club. I'm not sure she thinks Father should have. But I'm glad he did, because now I KNOW we'll stay, no matter what. At least I think I'm glad. I want to be glad.

April 24, 1935

A postcard from Floyd! Yippee! Mother let me keep it to put in my journal. This is the first mail I've ever got — and it's from Floyd!

DEAR EVERYBODY,
I T'S BEEN A REAL EYE-OPENER COMING OUT HERE. I THOUGHT THINGS WAS JUST BAD AT HOME, BUT THEY'S BAD EVERYWHERE! I'VE SEEN A CROWD OF 50 GROWN MEN FIGHT OVER A BARREL OF GARBAGE OUTSIDE THE BACK DOOR OF A RESTAURANT — 50 MEN FIGHTING OVER SCRAPS FIT FOR A DOG!
WHEN I HOPPED THE TRAIN, THEY WAS ALREADY A CROWD OF KIDS IN IT. SEEMS LIKE THE WHOLE COUNTRY'S ON THE MOVE, LOOKING FOR BETTER TIMES. ONE KID, SPIT, HAD BEEN "ON THE RODS" (THAT'S RIDING THE RAILS) FOR A YEAR. HE GAVE ME TIPS ON HOW TO AVOID THE "RAILROAD BULLS" (THAT'S COPS), HOW TO "PIPE THE STEM" (THAT'S ASK FOR A HANDOUT), AND WHERE TO "BUNK" (THAT'S SLEEP). I'VE GOT A LOT TO LEARN, BUT I'M LEARNING.   FLOYD

1¢
ROOFING

THE SAMUELS
RURAL ROUTE 1
KEOTA, KANSAS

I read this card about twenty times, but it still didn't tell me what I wanted to know — where is he now and how is he doing? If things are bad all over, is it better to be away from home? Does he miss us at all? Does he miss me?

April 30, 1935

This drought goes on and on. A rain cloud will hover on the horizon, the air will cool down, I'll even smell the rain coming, but it's only a promise that's quickly broken. No rain. No rain again.

With no wheat, no hay, no corn, Father couldn't feed the cattle anymore. There was nothing for it but to sell them, even though prices are low, since so many other farmers are also forced to sell. He took to market the 63 cows we had left. And no one would buy them — they were too thin! Father wouldn't let them starve, so he took all the money he'd saved for the bank and bought $50 worth of feed to fatten them up. Today he took the cattle back to the market, and he could finally sell them — for all of $51.60. All that work for a profit of $1.60! Floyd was right — farming is no way to make a living!

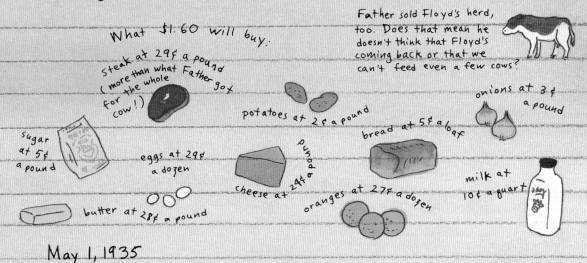

What $1.60 will buy:

Father sold Floyd's herd, too. Does that mean he doesn't think that Floyd's coming back or that we can't feed even a few cows?

Steak at 29¢ a pound (more than what Father got for the whole cow!)

potatoes at 2¢ a pound

onions at 3¢ a pound

bread at 5¢ a loaf

sugar at 5¢ a pound

eggs at 29¢ a dozen

cheese at 24¢ a pound

oranges at 27¢ a dozen

milk at 10¢ a quart

butter at 28¢ a pound

May 1, 1935

There's a man come to town who said he could make it rain by setting off explosions. All the farmers (except Father, who has nothing to give) pooled theiry money to pay for nitroglycerin so he could explode the clouds into raining. There was a lot of booming, but no rain. That makes 3½ years of drought.

May 8, 1935

The rainmaker tried one last time and this time it worked! Today was the first rain since last fall! But it was a short rain, not enough to help the crops, not enough to fill the rain barrel, not enough to soak the earth and keep the dust from blowing away. Only enough for me to dance in.

I let the rain run down my face and into my mouth. It didn't last near long enough, but I relished every single drop.

Dusty jumped around, yapping. she'd never seen rain in all her life!

May 9, 1935

When I slopped the hogs this morning I found a boy sleeping in the barn. He was skinny and dirty, skittish as a jackrabbit. I told him not to worry, I'd get him something to eat. I was afraid he'd be gone by the time I got back with some steamed bread, but he was still there. He wolfed down the food and said he'd been hopping freights, just like Floyd! I had a hundred questions to ask, but I didn't get any answers. When the food was gone, so was the boy. I sure hope Floyd's been eating better than that. I hope he finds kindly people to feed him.

May 10, 1935

Here I was, worrying about Floyd, and today we got another postcard from him!

DEAR FAMILY,
  I'VE BEEN TO LOTS OF CITIES NOW, SLEPT IN LOTS OF HOBO JUNGLES, EATEN IN LOTS OF SOUP KITCHENS. IT'S NOT A BAD LIFE, BUT I DON'T WANT TO BE A HOBO FOREVER, LIKE SOME OF THESE KIDS. MY NEXT STOP IS NEW YORK CITY AND I WON'T BE A BUM NO MORE BUT A COMIC STRIP ARTIST.
  LAST NIGHT AS WE GOT OFF THE TRAIN, THE SHERIFF WAS WAITING FOR US. HE TOOK US TO JAIL, WHERE HE FED US BOILED POTATOES, TOMATOES, AND A SLICE OF STALE BREAD. IN THE MORNING, BEFORE HE PUT US ON THE NEXT TRAIN OUTTA TOWN, WE GOT A CUPFUL OF WATERY CORNMEAL MUSH WHILE THE REAL PRISONERS WERE FED A FEAST OF EGGS, BUTTERED TOAST, OATMEAL WITH MILK AND SUGAR, AND REAL COFFEE. I GUESS IF I WANNA EAT WELL, I GOTTA COMMIT A CRIME!

FLOYD

THE SAMUELS
RURAL ROUTE 1
KEOTA, KANSAS

I wanted to write to Floyd and tell him about the rain (something is better than nothing), that now he can come back home, but he didn't give an address. Who knows — by now he could be in New York City. Father said Floyd will come home as soon as he learns how tough cities can be. Spending a night in jail sounds tough enough to me already.

I've seen pictures of New York in the newspaper, and it's all tall buildings. You can't see the land, and the sky is chopped up into small pieces by the skyscrapers. (To me, they're sky-shredders!) I'd hate it there. I worry about Floyd in such an awful place, even if he can draw comics there.

May 12, 1935

The rain was far too little, far too late. The bank is foreclosing on our farm. Father was counting on the sale of the cattle to pay the mortgage, but $1.60 wasn't enough to satisfy the bank.

There was a meeting of the Last Man's Club at Mr. Hodges' house. The members told Father not to worry — they wouldn't let him down. Father should stay on his land and farm it, like he'd sworn to do, and no one was going to kick him off of it.

I thought I wanted to leave this place, but now that it's being taken from us — now that we have no choice — I can't bear the idea of going.

Little green shoots are everywhere now, fed by the recent rain. The air smells fresh and grassy again, not gray and gritty, and the flat land brings the sky closer. White cottony clouds fill the blue.

May 13, 1935

Mother and Father entered a dance contest today, like the one on the radio. This one's over in Sandy Springs. My parents aren't dancers — leastwise, I've never seen them dance. But it doesn't matter. The prize money of $50 goes to whoever dances the longest, not the best. Mother is excited they might win. She even wore her best Sunday dress. Father looked handsome in Grampa's old suit. I wanted to watch them, but I have to take care of the farm. Me! All by myself!

May 14, 1935

I never knew how big our house was until I had to sleep in it all by myself. First Pearl left, then Floyd, now Mother and Father. Only of course Mother and Father will come back. Maybe with the money we need to save the farm.

May 15, 1935

Mother and Father are still dancing. Thirtytwo couples started the contest, and twelve have already dropped out. Grampa came by with the news. He brought me some biscuits and a jar of Gramma's jam.

The house was very quiet after Grampa left. I want Mother

The warmed-up biscuits and jam were delicious, but most of all, I just liked having Grampa sit at the kitchen table and talk with me.

and Father to win. But I want them home with me, too.

I'm not supposed to let Dusty on my bed, but it was a comfort to have her there last night. I'll only let her stay there until Mother and Father come home.

May 16, 1935

A loud BUMP woke me up last night. I sure wished Father was home then. What could I do all by my lonesome? Dusty ran to the door, barking like crazy, and even though I just wanted to hide my head under the pillow, I followed her outside to the henhouse. The other dogs were barking, too, but I didn't see them anywhere. Then I realized I must have shut them in the barn by mistake. That meant nothing was guarding the chickens! If Mother came home to find her henhouse empty, it would really be the last straw. And it'd be all my fault!

I ran to the henhouse, scared of what I'd see. The chickens were all aflutter, and two eyes gleamed out at me. A wolf? No, it was a fox! Dusty chased after it, but I was afraid the fox would hurt <u>her</u>, so I ran after the both of them. That fox hightailed it out of there, but I was shaking when I went back to free the dogs and check on the hens. It was a miracle, but none of the chickens were harmed, just a few eggs broken.

I sat in the moonlight and cried. I'd promised Father to take care of the farm. I'd let him down, but it wouldn't happen again. As long as this farm is ours, I'd try to be as good a farmer as he is.

May 17, 1935

Grampa came by with cornbread and the latest dance news. Eight couples are left, including Mother and Father. Could they win? I sure hope so!

And we got another letter from Floyd! It's good to hear from him, but I'm worried that if we're kicked off the farm, he won't know where to write to us and _we_ can't find _him_. This could be the last letter we get.

So Floyd likes New York. If we have to leave, maybe we should go there. Then we'd have a chance of finding him again. But Father's a farmer, so we'd probably go to California, like Pearl.

DEAR FAMILY,

THANKS TO THE HOBO CODE, I HAD MY FIRST <u>REAL</u> MEAL IN WEEKS. IF YOU SEE THIS CHALK MARK ON A DOOR 🐱, IT MEANS A KINDLY LADY LIVES THERE — AND KINDLY THIS ONE WAS! JUST OUTSIDE OF NEW YORK, I JUMPED OFF THE TRAIN BECAUSE I WAS STARVING. I JUST <u>HAD</u> TO FIND SOMETHING TO SCOFF. LUCKY FOR ME, THE FIRST HOUSE I COME TO HAD THAT CAT ON IT, AND I WAS TREATED TO FRIED CHICKEN, DUMPLINGS AND GRAVY, AND FRESH HOT BISCUITS. THE NICE LADY EVEN WRAPPED UP A THICK TURKEY SANDWICH FOR ME TO TAKE WITH.

SO I WAS FEELING GOOD WHEN I HIT NEW YORK. WHAT A CITY! I THOUGHT CHICAGO WAS BIG, BUT NEW YORK IS REALLY SOMETHING! EVEN WITH LONG BREADLINES AND PARK BENCHES FULL OF UNWASHED UNEMPLOYED MEN, THIS PLACE FEELS ALIVE. I HAD TO SPEND MY FIRST NIGHT SLEEPING IN AN UNLOCKED CAR, BUT I CAN TELL THIS IS THE PLACE FOR ME!

FLOYD

May 18, 1935

Three couples are still dancing, but Mother and Father came home today. I wanted to cry when I saw them. I know I wanted them here, but I wanted them to win more.

Mother's eyes are so sad now. She's given up — there's no hope left in her.

Mother's sorting through things, deciding what to take and what to leave behind. Father was angry when he saw what she was doing. He still won't give up - not yet, not ever — and he doesn't want her to, either. He's counting on the Last Man's Club to help him but what can they do? They're just drought-stricken farmers like him. No one's got much money.

Gramma and Grampa came over today. They want us to stay with them, but what about Uncle Victor? The farm is supposed to be his one day. Father's too proud to depend on others, even family. He hasn't taken any Relief money, and he's not going to start begging now. (Bad enough that Floyd's doing that!)

Father's eyes are hard and set. It's not hope he has but a fierceness. He won't give up.

Now when I see bindle stiffs on the road, I think of Floyd — they always look so tired and hungry. Father hates the idea that his son has gone from farmer to hobo. I hate the idea that Floyd could be starving.

May 20, 1935

I look in the mirror, and I don't know what I feel. I want to be strong like Father, but part of me is afraid Mother's right.

Floyd must know we're thinking of him because we got another letter today! He sure sounds happy. And he's not a hobo or a beggar anymore — he even sent money! Mother cried when she saw it. Father just grumbled it wasn't near enough.

DEAR FAMILY,
GREETINGS FROM YOUR SON, THE ARTIST! MY SECOND
DAY IN NEW YORK, MY STOMACH WAS EMPTY AND GROWLING,
SO I WENT INTO A SALOON AND OFFERED TO DRAW ON
THE WINDOW ANY KIND OF PICTURE THE OWNER WANTED.
I TOLD HIM IT WOULD BE GOOD ADVERTISING AND I
POINTED OUT ALL THE OTHER JOINTS WITH PAINTED
WINDOWS. HE SAID YES! I CLEANED THE WINDOW AND DREW:

A FOAMING STEIN
OF BEER

A HAPPY
CUSTOMER

A DACHSHUND
BEGGING FOR
BONES

THE OWNER WAS SO PLEASED, HE FED ME AN
ENORMOUS DINNER AND GAVE ME 50¢! SEE, FATHER,
DRAWING CAN FILL YOUR BELLY.
BUT THAT'S NOT ALL. I FELT SO GOOD, I DARED TO RING
THE DOOR OF BUGGY BITTO — YOU KNOW, THE FELLER
WHO WRITES AND DRAWS "BITTO DITTO." IT WAS A VERY
FANCY PLACE, AND A MAID ANSWERED THE DOOR AND HAD
ME WAIT IN THE PARLOR. I WAITED AND WAITED SOME
MORE AND WAS ABOUT TO GIVE UP AND GO WHEN BUGGY
BITTO HISSELF CAME IN. I SHOWED HIM MY COMICS AND
ASKED IF I COULD WORK FOR HIM, INKING HIS STRIP.
TURNS OUT HE'S STARTING A NEW PROJECT — A WHOLE
MAGAZINE OF NOTHING BUT COMICS! — AND HE COULD
USE THE HELP. HE LIKED MY DRAWINGS SO MUCH,
HE HIRED ME TO PENCIL AND INK! I'M EARNING $15
A WEEK — CAN YOU BELIEVE IT? I'M SENDING YOU MY
FIRST $5. MORE TO COME!   FLOYD

May 23, 1935

Five dollars or no five dollars, the bank foreclosed today, and the auction is set for tomorrow. We don't own anything anymore, not even Dusty. The bank says it all belongs to them and will be sold off to the highest bidder.

I rode Flit one last time, all over the Big Pasture and down past the Back Acre. I wanted to say good-bye to every inch of our farm. I said good-bye to the chickens (I saved them from a fox but not from the bank!), the horses, the dogs, and to Dusty last of all. I have 12¢ of my own money. Maybe that will be enough so I can buy Dusty back.

It was beautiful and clear today, as if to make sure I understand what I'm losing. The dust is still mounded around the fence posts, but the green sprouting everywhere promises a better time to come. Only I won't be here to see it.

May 24, 1935

I thought April 14 was a Black Day because of the dust storm, but today is blacker. Father who <u>never</u> loses hope, looks lost today. Mother's staying here, packing up, but I'm going into town with Father for the auction. I aim to keep Dusty no matter what.

May 24, 1935 (later)

It started out a Black Day but ended in a miracle! Father was right — the Last Man's Club saved us!

When we got to the courthouse, it was packed with farmers — mostly folks we knew, but some we didn't. When the bidding started, Mr. Hodges gave the first bid of a nickel for our farm. The judge called for another bid, calling it a ridiculous price for land like ours, but no one said a word, and Mr. Hodges' bid won. So it went the rest of the day — our horses sold for 10¢ each, the hayer, plow, harness, tools for a total of $3.00. And when Dusty was put up for sale, I bought her for 2¢! I even had money left over to buy Rags and the chickens. The whole of Father's $800 mortgage was settled for $5.35. That is, the other farmers (and me with my 12¢) paid the bank $5.35, and then Father turned around and bought our farm back from them using Floyd's $5. (Father was wrong — Floyd's money <u>was</u> enough!)

Mr. Hodges

Mr. Sorenson

Grampa

Father

Me

The Last Man's Club
(and one Last Girl)

Mr. Faber

Mr. Fergis

Mr. Dowling

All the kitchenware went for 3¢.

Even the broom was sold.

It was all done quietly and seriously. At first the judge looked angry, but as the sale went on, he seemed to think it the funniest thing. When the last pot was auctioned off, he slammed down his gavel and said, "Sold — and justice is done!"

Mr. Hodges said he'd heard of lots of farmers bidding this way to keep the land with its rightful owners. Some judges weren't as nice as ours, though, and had to be threatened with the sight of a noose. One judge was so mean, the farmers grabbed him from the courthouse and drove him out of town to a country road. They couldn't decide whether to really hang him or drag him behind a track for a while. In the end, they just dumped a hubcap full of grease on his head, stripped off his clothes, and left him there buck naked in the middle of nowhere.

a right honorable judge

Tonight we had a big celebration. The farmers all came home with us, bringing their families. Some brought waffles, others fried chicken, still others biscuits. Mother was dancing in the kitchen from the news, her cheeks pink with happiness. She opened up preserves and whipped up berry cobblers to finish off our feast. I ate until my stomach was tight and round, but the best part was just being with everyone, seeing everyone smile and joke. It felt like home again. So many people have

Mother was her old self, smiling and gossiping with the neighbors, swapping make-do recipes for milk gravy and buttermilk pie.

In all the gray, I found a few wildflowers. Usually the fields are covered with them by now— today it's a miracle to find any.

moved away, Keota has been a dying town, but tonight it was alive.

June 3, 1935

It's hot as the dickens today, as dry and dusty as ever, but now that the farm's really ours and no one can ever take it away, it doesn't seem to matter as much. I must have caught a dose of Father's hope— the farmer's habit of always thinking tomorrow will be better. Mother's caught it, too. She's singing again, even though we're still eating beans and corn bread and still battling the constant invasion of dust. Maybe there'll be an end to this drought after all. Maybe soon.

June 10, 1935

Floyd sent more money today, along with a letter and a copy of his comic strip. (It's his even if his name's not on it.) Finally he gives an address, too, so we can write back. There's so much to tell!

DEAR EVERYONE,
I'M SENDING YOU MY FIRST PRINTED STRIP. ISN'T IT A BEAUTY? I MISS YOU ALL, BUT I REALLY FEEL LIKE I BELONG HERE. PEOPLE THINK CITY FOLK ARE COLD AND MEAN, BUT THAT'S NOT SO AT ALL. I WAS EATING IN A DINER WHEN A WOMAN CAME IN AND ORDERED A BOWL OF SOUP. SHE GULPED IT DOWN AND TOOK OUT A NICKEL TO PAY FOR IT. THE COUNTERMAN SAID, "IT'S A DIME FOR SOUP," AND THE WOMAN STARTED TO CRY. THAT'S ALL THE MONEY SHE HAD, YOU SEE, AND SHE HADN'T MEANT TO TAKE WHAT SHE COULDN'T PAY FOR. THE COUNTERMAN DIDN'T GET MAD, THOUGH. HE JUST SIGHED AND SET A SLICE OF PIE IN FRONT OF HER. "HERE," HE SAID, "YOU MAY AS WELL OWE ME FOR THIS, TOO." THIS IS A CITY WITH A HEART!

FLOYD

Floyd's such a good artist! It's funny to think that people all over the country are looking at his pictures. Maybe even Pearl will see them!

When Father read this strip he didn't say anything, but I saw a smile flit across his face. I bet Father's as proud of Floyd now as I am.

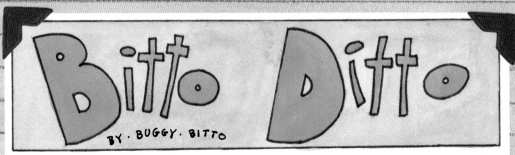

Bitto Ditto

BY · BUGGY · BITTO

I'S SHORE HONGRY!

HOWDY, MA'AM. GOT A JOB I COULD DO FOR A HUNK O' BREAD 'N' CHEESE?

BEATIN' RUGS BEATS STARVIN'!

IT'S A LONG HARD ROAD GOING FROM FARMHOUSE TO FARMHOUSE...

BUT THE WHISTLE OF A TRAIN IN THE DISTANCE GIVES BITTO AN IDEA — SHOULD HE HEAD FOR THE BIG CITY?

June 16, 1935

    Father took me to the store today, and we bought sorghum
seed with Floyd's money. Usually we plant wheat and corn, but Father
says now the government will pay farmers to sow sorghum and grass
instead because those crops will feed the soil so it won't dry up and
blow away. It seems all the years of planting the same thing over
and over again wasn't good for the land. That's why it turned to
dust and blew away.

Father talked to me like
he used to talk to Floyd—
not like I was a little
girl who wouldn't
understand
anything.

    I liked Father explaining
these things to me, as if I
were a farmer, too, and
that's when I knew it —
I knew I'd take over the farm from Father. Floyd belongs to the
city, but I belong to this farm — and someday it's gonna belong
to me. I took care of it all by myself for six days, I can do it
for the rest of my life. There'll be droughts and hard times.
That's the farming life. But there's always good times ahead
and neighbors you can count on, like the Last Man's Club. That's
the farming life, too. And that's what I want my life to be.

    Even Dusty looks like she's smiling these days.
She knows where she belongs, and so do I.

The author gratefully acknowledges the kind assistance of the Library of Congress in researching the cover photograph, which is from its photo archive. In addition, the author would like to thank the Bancroft Library at the University of California at Berkeley, which was of great assistance in researching *Rose's Journal* and which provided all interior photographs from its collection.

www.HarcourtBooks.com

First Silver Whistle paperback edition 2003

Silver Whistle is a trademark of Harcourt, Inc., registered in the United States of America and/or other jurisdictions.

Library of Congress Cataloging-in-Publication Data
Moss, Marissa.
Rose's journal: the story of a girl in the Great Depression/by Marissa Moss.
p.   cm.—(Young American Voices)
"Silver Whistle."
Summary: Rose keeps a journal of her family's difficult times
on their farm during the days of the Dust Bowl in 1935.
1. Depressions—1929—Kansas—Juvenile fiction.   2. Dust storms—Kansas—Juvenile fiction.
[1. Depressions—1929—Fiction.   2. Dust storms—Fiction.   3. Farm life—Kansas—Fiction.
4. Family life—Kansas—Fiction.   5. Kansas—Fiction.   6. Diaries—Fiction.]   I. Title.   II. Series.
PZ7.M8535Ro   2001
[Fic]—dc21   00-63466
ISBN 0-15-202423-9
ISBN 0-15-204605-4 (pb)

LEO   10 9 8 7 6
4500284684

The illustrations in this book were done in watercolor, gouache, and ink.
The text type was hand-lettered by Marissa Moss.
The display type was set in Bertie.
Color separations by Bright Arts Ltd., Hong Kong
Production supervision by Sandra Grebenar and Wendi Taylor
Designed by Steve Lux and Rose

Author's Note

Anyone who lived through the Great Depression had the experience permanently imprinted on them. My grandparents saved _everything_ — scraps of tinfoil, rubber bands, bits of cardboard — because you never knew when something would be useful. They were experts at "making do," transforming cardboard into shoe soles, scrap metal into candlesticks.

Researching the Depression introduced me to history that was both familiar and completely unknown. The extent and depth of misery was compounded by natural disasters of biblical scale — dust storms and a ten-year drought in the plains, flooding in the south. Bad situations grew into horrific ones, and it was all richly documented by writers and photographers on the Federal payroll and by that newest of media, cinema, in numerous black-and-white newsreels. I'm particularly indebted to the media collection of the University of California at Berkeley and to the following books (among many others): Ann Marie Low's Dust Bowl Diary, T. H. Watkins's _The Hungry Years_, Thomas Minehan's _Boy and Girl Tramps of America_, David Burg's _The Great Depression_, Erskine Caldwell's _You Have Seen Their Faces_, and of course, John Steinbeck's _Grapes of Wrath_. The Bancroft Library at UC, Berkeley gave me access to its impressive collection from the Farm Security Administration, and the photos in _Rose's Journal_ all come from the Bancroft, with the exception of the picture on the cover, which is from the Farm Security Administration collection in the Library of Congress.

In _Rose's Journal_ I tried to include various aspects of the Depression — contemporary news (like Bruno Hauptmann's trial for kidnapping the Lindbergh baby), popular culture, rural poverty, city breadlines, and the thousands of young people hopping freight trains in search of better lives. The 1930s were the heyday of radio and of big movie musicals. No matter how poor, nearly everyone could spare a quarter for an occasional evening of complete escapism. (If you were a kid, you could go to the Sunday matinee for a mere nickel — and maybe win a door prize to boot!) The '30s were also when the popularity of comic strips grew to the point that a novel format was invented — the comic book. Superman and his adventures first appeared then, joining Flash Gordon and Buck Rogers. Many of these comics were inked and drawn by teenage boys much like Floyd.

The events Rose describes are all true (even the exchange of a meal for painting decorations on a barroom window). Keota, Kansas, was a real place (see Bill Ganzel's _Dust Bowl Descent_), a small farm community of two hundred or so. But by the end of the Depression, only two families were left. I like to think Rose's was one of them.

Other exciting titles by Marissa Moss in the Young American Voices series:

Rachel's Journal: *The Story of a Pioneer Girl*

Traveling by covered wagon, young Rachel and her family follow the Oregon Trail from Illinois all the way to California. The terrain is rough and the seven-month trip is filled with adventure. Rachel's own handwritten journal chronicles every detail as she and her family make their way to their new home in California.

Emma's Journal: *The Story of a Colonial Girl*

The year is 1774, and the American Revolution for independence from the British is underway. Emma wants desperately to help the American struggle for freedom. When Papa gives her a secret code the militia uses, Emma finally gets her chance to change the course of history.

Hannah's Journal: *The Story of an Immigrant Girl*

America! Hannah's small European village buzzes with tales of life free from persecution—a place called America. Timid cousin Esther has passage for two aboard a ship bound for New York, and Hannah convinces Mama and Papashka to let her use the extra ticket. Will America really be everything they've ever dreamed of?

Marissa Moss is best known for her handwritten and illustrated journals, including those in the Young American Voices series. She also writes and illustrates the wildly popular *Amelia's Notebook* series, including *Amelia's Notebook, Amelia Writes Again, Amelia Hits the Road,* and *Amelia Takes Command.* Ms. Moss lives in Berkeley, California.